WEDDING BELLS FOR R⦿TTEN RALPH

Written by Jack Gantos

Illustrated by Nicole Rubel

HarperCollins*Publishers*

The character of Rotten Ralph was originally created by Jack Gantos and Nicole Rubel.
Text copyright © 1999 by Jack Gantos. Illustrations copyright © 1999 by Nicole Rubel. Printed in the U.S.A. All rights reserved.
Library of Congress Cataloging-in-Publication Data • Gantos, Jack. • Wedding bells for rotten Ralph / written by Jack Gantos ;
illustrations by Nicole Rubel. • p. cm. • Summary: Sarah's high-spirited, poorly behaved cat, Ralph, disrupts her aunt's wedding
with his outlandish antics. • ISBN 0-06-027533-2. — ISBN 0-06-027534-0 (lib. bdg.) • [1. Cats—Fiction. 2. Behavior—Fiction.
3. Weddings—Fiction.] I. Rubel, Nicole, ill. II. Title. • PZ7.G15334Wc 1999 • 98-27024 • [E]—dc21 • CIP AC
1 2 3 4 5 6 7 8 9 10 ❖ First Edition. Visit us on the World Wide Web! http://www.harperchildrens.com

One morning when Sarah woke up, Rotten Ralph was driving his monster truck across her bed. "Ralph," she said, "it's Aunt Martha's wedding day, and we have to get ready."

"I want to stay home and play," Ralph said to himself.

Sarah gave Ralph a little basket. "I'm the flower girl," she said. "Please fill this with fresh rose petals."

Rotten Ralph was happy to help. He went into the garden and put slugs and snails and toads in the basket.

When he went back inside, Sarah had another
job for him. "Take these dishes and wrap them
up for Aunt Martha's wedding gift," she said.
Rotten Ralph put the dishes in his monster

truck and zoomed around the living room.

"Whoops," he said when he crashed. He quickly

loaded the pieces in a smelly pizza box and tied

the ribbon in a big knot.

"Time to stop playing with your truck and get cleaned up," said Sarah. She gave Ralph a bath. Then she dressed him in some wedding clothes. "You look so handsome," she said.

When they arrived at the church, Sarah showed
Ralph to his seat. "Now just sit still and watch
the wedding," she said. But Ralph couldn't see a
thing. He hopped over the pews and knocked
all the tall hats off the ladies. "Now I'll be able
to see," he said to himself.

When the wedding started, Sarah hurried up
the walkway and threw rose petals from her
basket. Rotten Ralph winked at her as everyone
was covered with slugs and snails and toads.

Next, the little ring bearer slowly marched up the aisle. He tripped over Ralph's tail, and the rings rolled all the way to the front of the church. Rotten Ralph smiled.

"Ralph," whispered Sarah, "keep your tail to yourself."

Everyone stood as the bride entered the church.
When she passed Rotten Ralph, he pounced
onto her train and rode it up to the altar.

"This is better than riding a monster truck," he thought to himself. But Sarah was very upset. She waved for him to get off. Ralph smiled and waved back.

Once the wedding vows were read, the minister said, "It is now time for the bride and groom to kiss."

Rotten Ralph snatched the church mouse and held it between their lips.

"Yuck," Aunt Martha shouted after the kiss. "I married a mouse, not a man."

At the reception, Ralph had lots of fun. He helped the photographer capture every special moment.

He danced wildly with Sarah. He swung her around. He stepped on everyone's toes.

"Slow down," Sarah cried. "You're making me dizzy."

When the bride and groom went to cut the
cake, someone had gotten to it first.

"I bet I know who did that," Sarah said to
herself. She peeked under the table and caught
Ralph eating a monster slice of cake.

When Ralph finished eating, he felt sick.

He stumbled around the reception and knocked
over the tent stakes.

Finally, the bride and groom were ready to drive away. Aunt Martha tossed the bouquet over her shoulder.

"I hope I can catch it," Sarah thought.

But she didn't.

Someone else did.

On the way home, Sarah was sad. "You were so rotten," she said.

"Remember, someday you might get married and you'll want everyone to be nice to you."

"I'm sorry," thought Ralph. "I was just trying to have a good time."

When they got home, Rotten Ralph jumped up onto Sarah's lap and surprised her with the bride's bouquet. "Oh, Ralph," cried Sarah. "Does this mean you love me more than your monster truck?"

Rotten Ralph purred. "Maybe," he thought. And then he fell asleep.